the secret footprints

by julia alvarez

illustrated by fabian negrin

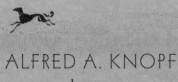

ALFRED A. KNOPF

new york

For Laurita,
ciguapita,
and for all those ciguaponas and ciguapitas
who use their spunk
in the service of their communities!
—J.A.

To Pam and Joanna, Fausta and Paolo
—F.N.

My gracias
to Carol Chatfield, children's librarian at Ilsley Library,
who has introduced me to the treasures I missed in childhood;
to Tracy Mack, who helped me with earlier drafts of this story;
and finally, to Andrea Cascardi,
who saw it through to the finished draft.
¡May the ciguapas be with you!
—J.A.

THIS IS A BORZOI BOOK PUBLISHED BY ALFRED A. KNOPF

Text copyright © 2000 by Julia Alvarez
Illustrations copyright © 2000 by Fabian Negrin
All rights reserved under International and Pan-American Copyright Conventions.
Published in the United States of America by Alfred A. Knopf, a division of Random
House Inc., New York, and simultaneously in Canada by Random House of Canada
Limited, Toronto. Distributed by Random House, Inc., New York.
KNOPF, BORZOI BOOKS, and the colophon are registered trademarks of
Random House, Inc.
www.randomhouse.com/kids

Library of Congress Cataloging-in-Publication Data

Alvarez, Julia.
The secret footprints / by Julia Alvarez ; illustrations by Fabian Negrin.
p. cm.
Summary: A story based on Dominican folklore, about ciguapas, a tribe of beautiful
underwater people whose feet are attached backward, with toes pointing in the
direction from which they have come.
1.Taino Indians—Folklore. 2. Tales—Dominican Republic. [1. Taino Indians—
Folklore. 2. Indians of the West Indies—Dominican Republic—Folklore.
3. Folklore—Dominican Republic.] I. Negrin, Fabian, ill. II. Title.
F1090 .A47 2000
398.2'097293—dc21   99-042217

ISBN 0-679-89309-1 (trade)   0-679-99309-6 (lib. bdg.)

Printed in Singapore
September 2000

10 9 8 7 6 5 4 3 2 1
First Edition

On an island not too far away and in a time not so long ago lived a secret tribe called the ciguapas. They made their homes underwater in cool blue caves hung with seashells and seaweed. They came out on land to hunt for food only at night because they were so fearful of humans. Some ciguapas said they would rather die than be discovered.

Luckily, the ciguapas had a special secret that kept them safe from people. Their feet were on backward! When they walked on land, they left footprints going in the opposite direction.

That is how the ciguapas had kept their whereabouts unknown for so long.

But once, their secret was almost discovered.

In the tribe lived a young ciguapa who was very beautiful, with bright eyes and golden skin and black hair that flowed all the way down her back. Unlike the other ciguapas, she was not fearful of humans. That is why her name was Guapa, which means brave and bold, and also beautiful, in Spanish.

Sometimes Guapa set out hunting at night before it was really dark enough.

One night, she wandered too close to a house where the family was still awake. When she saw their laundry hung out to dry, Guapa tried their clothes on. "This one fits me!" she cried out in a loud voice, and lights came on in the dark house.

A boy opened the window. "*¡Hola!*" he called in a friendly way.
Guapa was curious about him. *What is it like to be a human
child?* she wondered. But she hurried away.

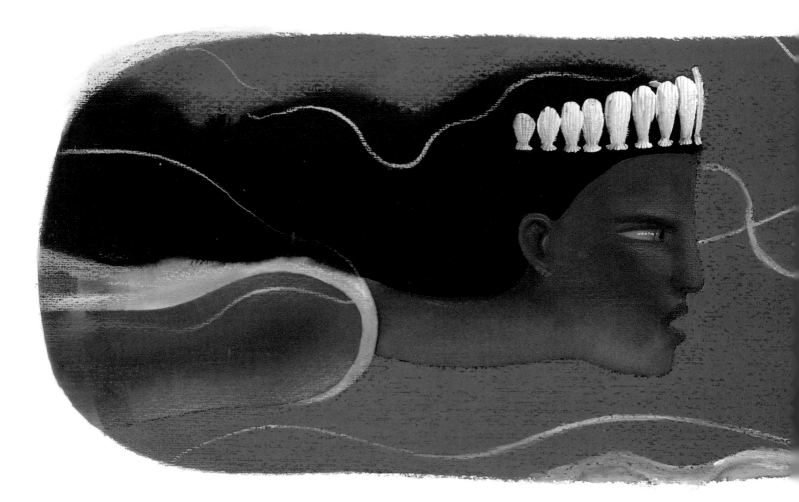

The tribe worried that Guapa's boldness might reveal their secret. They asked the queen to speak to her.

"Stop being such a mischief!" the queen ciguapa scolded her.

"But I'm bold and brave and curious about everything," Guapa said, defending herself. "That's why you named me Guapa, remember?"

"You must protect our secret," the queen said sternly.

"But why?" Guapa asked.

No ciguapa had ever dared ask the queen *that* question before.

The queen said, "If people find out where we live, they will capture us because we are so beautiful. Doctors will want to put us in cages and study us. We will be forced to live on land."

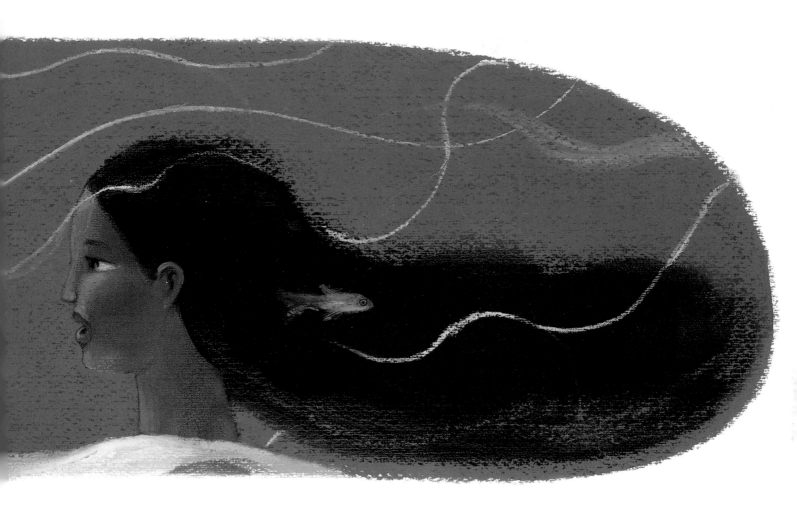

Guapa's mouth fell open. "¡Ay, no! I love living underwater, with fish tickling my neck and currents flowing through my hair so I never have to comb it. I don't want to live on land—I just like to visit!"

"Then you must stop taking chances," the queen warned. "Humans are unkind. They will force you to take baths and do laundry and wash your hands before meals."

That's when Guapa promised with all her heart that she would be very, very careful.

And she did work hard to keep her promise. She stayed underwater until it was dark, which was not always exciting. She followed behind everyone else in their food hunts, which was certainly frustrating. When she passed the clothesline at the boy's house, Guapa did not try the clothes on, which was no fun. She walked on tiptoes, which was not that easy for a ciguapa.

But one afternoon, Guapa forgot. She was looking up through the water at the sun sparkling like a thousand starfish in the sky. Up she came to the surface to take a closer look. It was that time of day when the island is most beautiful. The air seemed splashed with gold. Birds with feathers the colors of rainbows were practicing their favorite songs. Palm trees were swaying, as if they were listening to a catchy tune in the breeze. From the woods came the sweet smell of flowers.

Maybe the boy is out playing, she almost said out loud.

Guapa could not help herself. She climbed out of the water and started walking in the woods.

She came upon the family having a picnic under a shade tree by the river: the mother, the father, the boy, and his two little sisters.

Guapa hid behind some bushes and watched them eating fried *pastelitos* and mangoes from a basket on a large piece of cloth laid out on the grass. The sight made her hungry, *so* hungry. She had not eaten anything since the night before.

Soon the family got up for a walk. Guapa ran from her hiding place and snatched a snack from the leftovers in the basket.

The sound of the breeze stirring the leaves startled her. She turned
to run off, but she was not used to running on cloth. Down she came
with a loud thump!

Hearing the noise, the family turned around. "Are you all right?" they asked as
they ran to her side.

For once in her life, Guapa could not get a word out. The secret of the ciguapas
was going to be discovered! They would have to leave their cool blue caves at the
bottom of the river and live on dry land forever. Doctors would put them in cages
and stare at them. All because Guapa could not contain her curiosity.

"¡Ay, ay, ay!" she cried at the thought of such a disaster.

"She's really hurt," the boy said. "She can't walk."

"I'm afraid you're right, *mi'jo*," the father said, unwinding the cloth from around Guapa's feet. "She's twisted both her ankles badly."

"Does it hurt?" one of the two little girls asked. The other little girl was too little to think up her own question, so she also asked, "Does it hurt a lot?"

Guapa nodded. She would pretend that her ankles were twisted. No matter what, she would keep the secret of the ciguapas safe.

But then she heard the dreaded words. "We'd better take her to the doctor," said the mother. "He'll want to examine her."

"¡Ay, *ay, ay!*" Guapa cried when they tried to pick her up.

"We should not move her," the father said. "We should get the doctor and bring him here."

"We can't leave her alone," the mother said. By now it was dark in the grove beside the river.

"I'll stay with her," the boy said, puffing his chest out proudly.

The mother took the two little girls home to bed while the father
went for the doctor. "*Buenas noches,*" said the bigger little girl as they
left. "*Buenas noches,*" sang the littler little girl.

Guapa could hear whisperings, hoots, and soft whistles. She knew her
tribe of ciguapas was all around, hiding in the woods, waiting to see
what would happen, frightened that its secret had been given away.

The young boy was thoughtful. He stood guard beside Guapa. He
offered her another *pastelito* from the basket, and she gobbled it right
up. "Have more," he urged.

He put soft leaves under her head so she would be comfortable.

How nice of him, Guapa thought, smiling to herself.

"Is there anything else I can get you?" the boy asked her.

This was the chance she had been waiting for. "I could use some water,"
Guapa said. She was telling the truth. She needed something to wash down the
pastelitos that had gotten her into all this trouble.

"I'll bring you a coconut shell of water from the river," the boy said.
"But will you be all right by yourself?"

Guapa could not believe her good luck. "Oh, yes," she said. "*Sí, sí, sí.*" Around the grove a breeze ran through the trees. All the little leaves seemed to be whispering, "*Sí, sí, sí.*"

The minute the boy was out of sight, the ciguapas rushed out to carry Guapa away. "*Sh, sh, sh,*" the ciguapas said when Guapa tried to explain that she could walk on her own. She scooped up some *pastelitos* to show her ciguapa friends how kind the human boy had been. Then she left a seashell as a thank-you in their place.

When the boy came back, the beautiful young girl was gone.
But the strangest thing was that all the footprints in the sand
led back to the picnic spot. "These must be my family's tracks,"
he said, scratching his head.

When the tribe returned with Guapa and her delicious snacks, the queen ciguapa did not know what to say. "I suppose some human beings can be kind," she admitted.

Guapa would have answered, but her mouth was full.

Now, when the tribe wanders near the family's house, Guapa
is allowed to go right up to the windows and peek in.

Sometimes the boy goes walking in the woods, looking for
Guapa. He carries his lucky seashell in his pocket to remind him
of his mysterious friend.

Guapa has asked the ciguapas not to take any eggs from this family. When the laundry is left out, Guapa helps fold the clothes on the line for the kind boy and his two little sisters.

She always finds *pastelitos* waiting in the boy's pockets.

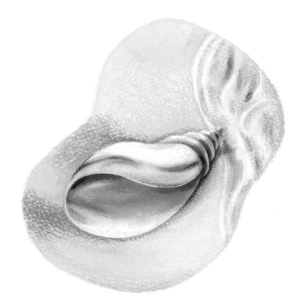

ABOUT THE STORY

I first heard about the ciguapas when I was as little as the littler little girl in my story. My family lived in the Dominican Republic, where the ciguapas come from. My mother and my aunts told me all about these beautiful creatures with golden skin and long black hair who live in caves under the water. I always thought it was so smart of them to have their feet on backward so their toes face where they have come from.

Now that I'm grown up and live in the United States, I've found that there are many different versions of the ciguapa story. These unusual and beautiful creatures originated a long time ago in the Dominican Republic. Some writers say they have golden skin, some say they have black skin. In some versions the ciguapas are very small, only about a yard tall, but in other versions they are as tall as human beings—in fact, they look just like us, except for their strange feet and their extraordinary beauty. Some say the ciguapas live in caves under the water, some say they live in caves in the woods. All the writers agree that the ciguapas only come out at night to hunt. In most versions of the story, the ciguapas are an all-female tribe, but in some versions there are male and female ciguapas. In the all-female stories, the ciguapas fall in love with human males and lure them away to their caves.

Some writers think the ciguapas came from the legends of the Taino Indians, who inhabited the island when Columbus and the Spaniards arrived in 1492. Others believe that the legend originated when the few Indians who were not killed by the Spaniards escaped to caves in the mountains and came out only at night to hunt for food. Since the Taino Indians had golden skin and black hair, maybe that is where the legend of the ciguapas came from.

Sometimes my mother and aunts would try to scare me at night by saying that if I didn't go to sleep quickly or if I turned on my light after lights-out, the ciguapas would come and take me away. They thought I would be scared, but I was secretly excited by the thought of seeing a ciguapa. I never did. Still, I haven't given up. Sometimes I leave my wash out on the line overnight and stick a piece of candy or an apple in the pocket of my pants or jacket, just in case. I know it's a long way from the Dominican Republic to Vermont, especially if your feet are on backward. But I have to tell you, sometimes that piece of candy or apple is gone from that pocket in the morning. My husband says it could be squirrels or maybe even a raccoon.

I know better.